TOMMY ON THE FARM

by

SOLVEIG
PAULSON
RUSSELL

illustrated by
ELFREDA

A WHITMAN TELL-A-TALE BOOK
Western Publishing Company, Inc., Racine, Wisconsin

WHITMAN and TELL-A-TALE are registered trademarks
of Western Publishing Company, Inc.

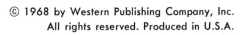

Tommy lived on a farm. He lived with his mother, father, and grandpapa. One day Grandpapa gave Tommy a tin horn and a toy drum.

"Now I can make music," Tommy said, and he hopped up and down and clapped his hands.

Tommy blew on his tin horn. *Toot-toot-toot-tee*. All around the farmyard he went, making music.

The farm animals listened and nodded their heads. Tommy's mother smiled.

Tommy put his horn under the apple tree. He picked up his toy drum. *Rub-a-dub-dub!* He marched around the tree, left-right, left-right.

All of the farm animals listened.
Tommy's father laughed.
Grandpapa said, "Music is wonderful.
Music makes Tommy a happy boy."

For one, two, three days Tommy blew the horn and beat the drum. On the fourth day rain suddenly came peppering down. Tommy ran to the house so fast he forgot the horn and drum.

Under the apple tree the tin horn filled with water. It rusted. The drumhead soaked up the rain.

When the sunshine came again, Tommy tried to blow the horn, but it only sputtered and squeaked.

He tried to beat the drum, but as soon as he hit the head it squashed down into the drum and tore in three places.

Tommy was sad. He put the horn and
the broken drum into the garbage can.

Then he climbed into the porch swing. "I have nothing to do," he said as he swung back and forth, back and forth, in a sorry, sad way. "I have no music!"

The turkey said, "Poor Tommy! He has no music. Music is so wonderful — Grand-papa said it makes Tommy happy. Could some of us make music for Tommy? I have a strong voice. I'll sing for him."

"We have good voices," said the ducks and geese.

"So have we," said the hens.

"Everyone knows my voice is famous," said the rooster. "I'll crow."

The cow, the horse, the donkey, the dog, the cat, and the pig all said, "We can sing! Very well!"

So all of the animals gathered to-gether in front of the porch. The turkey went, "Gobbledy gobble-gob!"

The ducks and the geese sang, "Quack quack, honk honk, squackledy-squack!"

The hens went, "Chuckledy chuck-chuck! Clackety-clackle!"

The rooster crowed, "Cock-a-doodle, doodle-doodle-doo!"

The dog barked, "Boof, whoof-bow! Wow-wow!"

The cat sang, "Meowder-ow! Meow!"

The pig grunted a deep "Oink oink oink, oink-honky-toink-boink!"

The horse went, "Whinnidy-winkledy-wink! Neigh-neigh! Neigh!"

The donkey went, "Hee-ee-haw-aw-aw! Haw!"

When Tommy heard all those sounds he jumped from the swing and clapped his hands and laughed and laughed.

"Ah, see!" said the gobbler. "Music *is* wonderful! Music makes Tommy happy!"

And after that whenever Tommy sat still for a little while with nothing to do, or if he couldn't find anything he wanted to play with, the turkey gobbler blinked wisely.

He strutted about, calling the other animals. "Cheer time! Cheer time!"

Then the animals gathered together and each one stood firmly, stretched his neck out far, and gave forth his best sounds for Tommy. Tommy liked it very much.

But Tommy's mother didn't like it. She cried, *"Ocht!* Such a racket! They make *frightful* sounds. They hurt my ears!" She tied two scarves tightly over her ears and wore a stocking cap over those.

Tommy's father said, "That's not singing! That's screeching. In fact, it's terrible!" He put on earmuffs and went off to sit in the farthest corner of the basement.

Grandpapa didn't like it. He pulled an old coat almost over his head and he sat in his rocking chair and did some thinking.

Then he pushed the coat aside, put on his hat, took his pocketknife from the shelf, and went down to the river where the willow trees grew.

He cut some tender willow shoots and took them home. He sat down and he whittled five whistles for Tommy. "Willows make good music," he said. "Music is wonderful. It makes Tommy happy. And when willow whistles get lost or broken I can make some more."

Tommy liked the
willow-whistle music.
*Tweet-tweet-twiddle-
dee-dee*. He sat
in a tree and
whistled.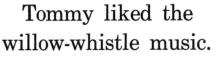

He lay in the tall
grass and tooted.

He marched around the yard with his whistle. And the animals listened, and marched sometimes, and nodded their heads because they loved Tommy.

"Tommy is happy with his music," said the watchful gobbler, "but it is nice to know that if Tommy needs OUR music, we can make it for him. Music is wonderful! It makes Tommy happy!"